I0556895

It is the Aeon of Chaos, a time of terror, wonder, and pleasures undreamed of. The gods are dead and the great demons gnaw at their bones. From the cannibal kingdom of Kaszanka to the sordid pornocracy of Thune life is frenzied and cheap. Fortunes and kingdoms are bartered at the swing of a blade. Lawlessness and lust rule the day, while magic and mayhem take charge of the night. Slavery and massacre swarm across the land like ants at a picnic, while notes of demon laughter dance over all like shadows of flames from the deific pyre. It is the Aeon of Chaos, and only Chaos reigns!

The Unwithering Flower

Copyright © 2021 by B.J. Swann

Editing by Christine Morgan

Cover by Elizabeth Bedlam

Punk AF and Aeon of Chaos Logos designed by Caelan Stokkermans Arts

The Unwithering Flower

R.J. Swann

Contents

7   Chapter 1: Dreams of Avarice

11   Chapter 2: The Stench of Opportunity

21   Chapter 3: The Unwithering Flower

29   Chapter 4: Closing Time

39   Chapter 5: Boys' Night Out

45   Chapter 6: Half-Mast

49   Chapter 7: Stiffs

55   Chapter 8: Frenzy

63   Chapter 9: Anti-birth

69   Chapter 10: Tales Within Tales

Chapter 1: Dreams of Avarice

It is the Aeon of Chaos. All the gods are dead, and the demons are adorned with their ashes.

Narseh stood grinning on the deck of the galley. He was a man of average height, with a swarthy complexion and a hawkish nose. The point of his manicured beard looked like the tip of a dagger in silhouette. He wore a saffron turban, a lime-green kaftan, and a set of jewelled slippers with crescent-shaped toes. A crescent-shaped dagger rested on his hip, continuing the motif.

The whole ensemble was typical in style for a man of his origins. Narseh came from Alhazred, the Land of Smokeless Fire, where rainbow flames dance across the desert at dusk, cold, silent, and scintillating, said to be stirred from the embers of the fire that had destroyed the old universe. Others said the flames were pieces of the ancient djinn, whose bodies lay scattered but yearning for life once again.

Narseh didn't care either way. He wasn't the romantic or sentimental type, and the unremitting grin he wore as his galley hugged the coastline was not one stirred up by memories of his homeland.

The coastline was rugged and dark. He could almost smell the wild goats as they frolicked and rutted on the mountains that rose from the water. It was a more pleasant scent than the stench of sweat and urine wafting from the galley's lower deck, where dozens of slaves sat toiling at the oars, chained to the benches and unable to rise, not even for the purpose of relieving their bladders.

The sound of their labour was a dull, dismal symphony. The shouting of the foreman and the cracking of his whip provided percussion; the groaning of the galley slaves provided a chorus; the creaking of the oarlocks and the sloshing of the waves were the song's sombre notes.

Yet neither was it the suffering of his chattel that made Narseh smile. He was not a cruel man, merely an indifferent one, and he would just as soon deal in happy slaves as in miserable ones – profit margins permitting, of course.

He glanced across the sea. Its glassy curves shimmered back at him like the facets of a poorly-cut diamond. For a moment he fancied himself standing atop such a gigantic gem, and tried to calculate the wealth he might gain from selling it – not all of it, of course, just fragments cut down into saleable portions. The rest he'd retain and transform into a house, a dazzling and transparent castle.

The fantasy, though pleasant, was not the reason for his grin. Such idle dreams of opulence flitted through his mind all day long, the way other men might fantasise about sex. Mere dreams of wealth could not move Narseh to smile, only its acquisition, actual or imminent.

As he kept watching the horizon, he finally caught sight of the cause of his joy – the port of Hedonia, City of Delights. Others called it simply the City of Whores. It lived up to either name, a coastal hub where sex was for sale in every conceivable variety.

Of course, many seaside towns focused on such trade. But

Hedonia was special. The people took their work very serious-ly. For them it was not merely some prosaic means of making money, but a discipline to be practised with all the application of alchemy. Ancient pleasure guilds trained their initiates in secret carnal arts long passed down through generations of chicken-heads and dynasties of prostate-ticklers. Thus the prostitutes of Hedonia had a singular reputation, and were to the whores of other regions as a regiment of knights to a rab-ble of conscripts.

They were the reason Narseh smiled. Not because he planned on having sex with any, of course; he never paid for anything he might get for free. No, he smiled because he planned to acquire some prostitutes and take them back to Al-hazred. He'd already liquidated a great deal of his assets in order to do so; the wealth was locked away in his hold in the form of a trunk full of diamonds, silver, and gold.

He could see it all now. He'd find himself a few good spec-imens of either gender, some young ones for beauty, some old ones for experience (though not too old, of course). Then he'd sail back to his homeland with his precious new cargo of hoes, where their value would quadruple. He could sell them off, or keep them and go into the whoremaster business himself, forcing his stable to divulge their carnal secrets to a slew of fresh initiates. He could start a Hedonia away from Hedonia, a franchise with a formula for ecstasy.

Yes, that was why Narseh was smiling, because he expected that soon – very soon – he'd be making a great deal of money.

The galley slowed as it drew towards the ramshackle jetties sprawling from the harbour. The sun sank redly above, tinting the vista the colour of blood. To Narseh it seemed as though he were staring through the facets of a gigantic ruby, taking in the city's slanted rooftops and flocks of circling pigeons.

There sure are a lot of pigeons, he thought.

Then he saw they weren't pigeons at all, but murders of crows. He inhaled through his nose to taste the fragrance of Hedonia, imagining a bouquet of perfumes to mask the scent of sex, but what he got instead was the stench of almighty decay, like a battlefield abandoned in summer to a conquering army of flies.

He inspected the port with horrified eyes. There were far fewer ships than he'd anticipated, and many of those were in the process of hastily departing. His limited view of the streets showed them mostly deserted, though they should've been bustling with bodies for sale. A single figure, dressed in a very un-revealing ensemble of black robes and leather mask in the likeness of a bird's beak, pushed a wheelbarrow filled with contents bundled and crooked and covered in a ragged black sheet. When the wheelbarrow jarred on a loose piece of paving, a body slipped out, buzzing with flies and fat with decay.

Oh fuck, thought Narseh. It's a plague!

Chapter 2: The Stench of Opportunity

Narseh felt like crying and tearing his beard out by the root. He'd come all this way, only to find the city riddled with plague. The prices of slaves would be vastly inflated. Worse yet, any chattel he purchased might be crawling with disease. They might die before he got them to Alhazred, or transmit their sickness to the galley slaves. Then he'd be sailing on a plague-ship, reeking not only of urine but of death. He might even end up having to row it himself!

The prospect was ghastly, so too the prospect of his own very possible demise. But both took a back seat to his fears about his finances.

Perhaps I should set sail immediately, he thought. *Just call the whole thing a loss!*

The very idea was anathema. Surely there was a way he could get a return on this venture! He stood on the deck, wracking his brains and staring at the hastily departing boats.

I've got it! he thought.

He could offer the unfortunate people of Hedonia an escape from the plague – for a price, of course. It wouldn't be as good as acquiring a hold full of specialised whores, but it might just allow him to recover the cost of his journey and make a little profit on top. He decided to go out in search of the wealthy and the desperate. Not in person, obviously – he'd send an expendable slave to do the rounds of the city in his stead, selling passage abroad.

It was a decent scheme. He no longer felt like crying, or tearing out his beard, though he was far from ecstatic. He was just about to go below deck and start putting his plan into action when he saw another galley pulling in besides his.

The vessel was silent, save for the groaning of oarlocks and the sloshing of oars in the surf. He heard no accompanying grunting of galley slaves, no clinking of chains, not even the rhythmical whipping of the lash against backs. The statue of a four-armed demon with the head of a bird and an onyx-black beak was mounted on the bow of the vessel. Surrounding it were pictograms littered with the macabre imagery of entrails, buzzards, and skeletons twisted into stylized shapes.

Such peculiar aesthetics proclaimed the ship as being from Khem, the land of the necromancers, who peopled their empire with animate dead.

The galley drew up along the jetty across from him, and a woman appeared on deck. She had a fine-featured face, with skin a shade darker than Narseh's. In spite of her beauty, Narseh's attentions were drawn not to her soft fulsome lips, nor to her cute button nose, but to the splendid-looking garments she wore. Her veil and matching dress were cut from dazzling silk in the colours of lapis and gold. Golden bits of jewellery encircled her wrists, ankles, and waist. The catches and buckles looked like serpents intertwisting and biting one other.

By contrast, one of her garments truly stood out from the others, not for its beauty, but for its utter repulsiveness. Hanging from her back, like a vulture's black plumage, was a cloak made from slivers of mortuary shrouds. Narseh could smell its foul odour even above the stench of the city. Its stitches were caked with the scum of decay, as though they'd been steeped in a cauldron of corpses. He recognised the garment as ritual garb, worn only by the necromancers of Khem. It served as a marker of their status, as well as a magickal fetish that helped steep their presence in the energies of death.

He nodded to the woman, smiling. He was always very friendly with strangers who looked very rich, and her jewellery alone was worth a small fortune. He wasn't sure exactly what he wanted from her yet, but the lustre of gold had him flitting to her presence like a bee to a pollinating flower.

"Greetings, fine lady," he hailed, concealing his disgust at her foul-smelling robe, as well as his general unease about necromancers, who had terrible powers he didn't understand. "Narseh Az-Pinah at your service. Merchant of the high seas."

He preferred not to say 'slaver of the high seas,' though that was the business he primarily engaged in. Slave-trading, unfortunately, had a bit of a branding problem, its practitioners viewed by many as sinister and grubby individuals. Some even thought the occupation was a crime against inherent human dignity! Total nonsense, in Narseh's opinion. Dignity wasn't inherent – you had to buy it, like everything else! Slaves couldn't buy and didn't own anything, ergo, no dignity for them. Hypothetically-speaking, even if they *did* possess dignity, their masters would technically own it all anyway, just as they owned their slaves' clothing, organs, and teeth. Still, it wasn't too much of a stretch to call himself a merchant; he'd buy and sell anything that might make him a profit.

The woman regarded him for a moment, long enough to have him wondering if perhaps she didn't speak Ozich.

Then she did reply. "Wena," she said. "Wena of Khem."

"A delightful name," said Narseh, "and one I must confess I've never heard before. So, Wena, what brings you to this perilous port? Here to buy corpses?" He knew the necromancers often did so, going abroad in times of catastrophe, seeking to plump up their empire's force of domestic undead.

In a way it made him jealous, the very idea there might be a form of labour even cheaper than slavery. If there was, then zombies were it. They didn't need to eat, sleep, or do any other things that cut into a man's bottom line. On the other hand, they couldn't reproduce, unlike living slaves, who could, would, and did, bringing forth a free generation of chattel, born into bondage from the very beginning. The fact that a stock of zombies could only be increased by the active collection of corpses was enough of a flaw in the whole necromantic operation to keep Narseh from weeping with jealously. Corpses weren't as easy to come by as might be imagined. Most people revered their dead loved ones, cremating their bodies with all due ceremony, and would rather jump on the pyre themselves than let the corpse of Dear Uncle Joe get transformed into a zombie. Thus, plague towns and other places where death was running rampant, where there weren't enough living to bury the dead, where bodies were disposed of in bulk by miserable corpse-carters who could easily be bribed to offer up their whole charnel inventory, proved ideal for the enterprising necromancer.

If that was Wena's purpose here, Narseh could see no conflict or intersection in their interests. After all, he had no corpses to sell – unless he wanted to slaughter his galley slaves, though he doubted the return would be worthwhile. Thus, he imagined he'd soon be bidding goodbye to this beautiful woman, and her beautiful gold.

"I'm not here for dead bodies," she said.

Does that mean she's here for live ones? wondered Narseh, looking her up and down again. She was a woman, after all, and he did sense a certain tender longing about her. Had she come to get ploughed by the gigolos of Hedonia?

It wasn't uncommon for wealthy ladies to engage in such sex tourism. The skills of the Hedonian man-whores were as legendary as those of their female counterparts, after all. As Narseh understood it from his research, many even bore coded tattoos on their biceps that spoke of their sexual abilities.

The image of a serpent stretched out between the sun and the moon, for instance, denoted the length of time they could maintain an erection. The longer the serpent, the longer the man-whore in question's crimson crowbar would stand at the ready. Certain rare specimens boasted the image of a serpent encircling sun and moon, meaning they were capable of keeping their meat in heat for a full day and night. Images of fruit or other foodstuffs, such as pineapples or mangoes, attested to the relative sweetness of their semen, as determined by a licensed tribunal of cum connoisseurs. The image of discrete grains of sand in an hourglass told of how long each had to wait after cumming before getting hard once again. Simple Ozich numerals – often running well into the double digits – indicated the number of climaxes each could reach in a day before being spent.

Additionally, the images of animals announced their affiliation among the Hedonian gigolo guilds, known for the size of their equipment or their mastery of certain techniques. The list of guilds included, he recalled, the Anacondas (no prizes for guessing their specialty); the Rhinos, whose members' members had a striking upward bend; and the Woodpeckers, who prided themselves not on length, nor on girth, but on speed of penetration. All such tattoos were inked in a similar style by licensed professionals. And woe to those who might try to lie through the use of illicit tattoos, for should their deception be uncovered, then their unlawful ink would be flayed from their bodies by the merciless Hedonian Sex Police.

Yes, Narseh knew all of these facts from his research on Hedonia. Yet, despite the great prowess – not to mention the freakish anatomical attributes – ascribed to the Hedonian hustlers, he couldn't see why a beautiful woman like Wena would pay for it. At least, not in her native land of Khem, where necromancy was normal and accepted; anywhere else, men might be repulsed by her profession, in spite of her looks. But in Khem she'd never run out of suitors, would have lovers aplenty – they'd be lining up around the block!

So what would she be doing in Hedonia, looking for some strange?

"Nor am I here for the gigolos, if that's what you're wondering," she added, seeming a little offended by his speculative perusal.

"I'm terribly sorry if my silence just now carried any untoward implications. But this is Hedonia, after all." He stepped down from his galley to the jetty between them, and after a brief pause she did likewise. Narseh bowed, took her hand, and kissed it gently, managing not to recoil from the morbid reek of her robe. "Might I ask, if you're not here for dead bodies – or live ones – what it is that you are doing here?"

"I'm in exile," she said. "They kicked me out with nothing but my galley, my jewels, and a couple of servants. Which means I have to make a living somehow. I thought here, where there's plague, my talents might prove lucrative."

"I didn't know necromancers could heal the sick," Narseh said.

"Oh, we can't. But we can use the Eyes of Death to see if there's sickness inside people. I can tell them if they've got the plague or not, for a modest fee."

As she stared at him, her beautiful emerald eyes became filmy and whitish, like those of the dead. Narseh shuddered under her scrutiny. Was she scanning him for plague, right then and there?

"Don't worry," she said as her eyes returned to normal. "You're healthy. Very healthy, in fact…"

For a moment, her gaze lingered lower than his eyes. Narseh almost didn't notice – he was too busy thanking the Candle King for his clean bill of health.

"Ah, yes, thank you for that free sample of your services," he said. "Tell me, though, have you ever tried this little scheme of yours before?"

"Well, no, not really…"

"I see. I'm afraid I've got some bad news for you: there's no way you'll make any money with it."

"Why not?"

Still suppressing his disgust at her putrescent cloak, Narseh put his arm around her shoulder in a comradely fashion, and gestured to the city around them.

"Think about it, my dear," he said. "If a person's feeling healthy, they're not going to *want* to know if they're sick or not.

All that matters to them is that they feel good right then, and they don't want to question that. They just want to go on living their lives, hoping everything will turn out all right. And the people who're *already* feeling ill? They don't need your services, because they already *know*! Which means you've no market to sell to, no market at all.'

"What about the local government?" she asked. "I could help them identify the sick ones, and put them in quarantine to stop the spread of the disease."

Narseh sighed, beginning to think her more than a little naïve. Whatever had they taught her at necromancy school? Certainly nothing about business or practical matters!

"Ah, Wena," he said. "You might be able to see with the Eyes of Death, but I see with Eyes of Gold Coins, and I'm afraid you're mistaken on that score as well. Those who run the government are probably already in hiding on their country estates, waiting it out. That's a fact I'd put money on, and I'm not a man who gambles lightly. Meanwhile, though, those very same masters of the city have their agents out in the streets, collecting their taxes as usual, taxes which've no doubt started dwindling most terribly, given all the death going on. So the *last* thing they'd want is to put a whole chunk of the city's population in quarantine. That'd diminish their revenues even further!"

"You mean they'd rather keep people working till they die?"

"Of course! Think about it. How long can a plague-ridden person walk around like normal, before the sickness goes and topples them over?"

Wena peered out into the streets, using her Eyes of Death to observe the vectors of plague moving about through the populace, bubbling like soup in people's organs and veins.

"A few days," she said. "Maybe a week, at the most."

"Exactly," said Narseh. "Just consider, all that labour lost. Hedonia has a twenty percent tax on prostitution, its primary industry. Imagine the thousands of whores who'd be put into quarantine for a week before they died. How many hand jobs and blow jobs and other sorts of jobs could they have done in that time, and all getting taxed at twenty percent? Then add in all the barbers, the stone masons, the mat weavers, the seamstresses, and so on. The rulers of the city would never agree to lose all that revenue, just to save on a few paltry lives. Let alone pay you for it. Trust me, I've dealt with a fair few governments in my time – monarchies, democracies, pornocracies, you name it. They all have one thing in common – they only ever care about cold, hard *cash*."

Wena sighed, perhaps realizing he might be correct.

"Well, I'm here now," she said. "There's got to be something I can do…"

At the sound of creaking footsteps behind them, Narseh whirled, coming face-to-face with a pair of Wena's servants, lugging her luggage down to the dock.

The servants were undead. That much was obvious, in spite of the cloaks they wore to disguise their true natures. They smelled of dried roses and preservatives, with just a hint of decay. Their desiccated bodies were wrapped in saffron silk winding sheets, their excavated eye sockets fitted with jewels. The finery was typical for the undead butlers of Khem's necromancer nobility, who liked to keep their servants attired in a manner that reflected the glory of their station. Even in exile, it seemed Wena liked to keep up appearances.

Narseh admired the jewels in the dead men's eyes, seeing his own face reflected in the facets. Oh how he loved to behold his own image in that beautiful environ of crystal! The sight often made him imagine a whole other world, a gemstone world, where his flesh was embodied in riches everlasting. But such fancies were not thoughts for today. No; today his mind was mired in the practical – and suddenly whirling with excitement.

He peered at the zombies, then back to the street, where a cartload of corpses was being offloaded from a brothel. His mercantile mind made a simple calculation, and he knew he had the answer, not just to his own monetary ambitions, but to Wena's want of gainful employment, as well. He couldn't believe he hadn't seen it right away!

"My marvellous Wena," he said with a smile, "I think this might be the start of a beautiful friendship!"

Chapter 3: The Unwithering Flower

A few months later…

Aktus wandered the streets of Hedonia, grumbling to himself as he went. The stench of death hung heavy in the air, but that wasn't why he was cranky. He was used to the aroma. He and his mercenary band, the Axes of Aarseth, had just spent six months fighting under contract for the kingdom of Myconia, helping them to conquer the neighbouring region of Pecoz.

Ah, the fighting had been fierce, the bodies piled ten-deep by the end of it, wafting up a death-reek even more potent than that of the city he strolled through at present. In the end, Myconia had won, and Aktus had made off like a bandit, not just with the agreed-upon payment for services rendered, but also with sacks of gold and goblets he'd plundered from Pecoz when "Havoc!" had been cried. Once all that had been done with, all he'd been able to think about was dipping his wick in the seasoned, sultry sybarites who dwelt in the legendary City of Whores.

Which led to his present ill-humour, for they'd arrived to find Hedonia in the wake of a plague, if not still being ravaged by some vestige of it. Many of the brothels remained shut. Those few whores out and about looked decidedly unhealthy, their bodies dotted with barely-healed buboes, their skin pale and sweaty in the glare of the lanterns that lit up the realm after dusk. Corpse-carts went rattling through the streets, oozing yet more stench as they carried off the last of a logjam of bodies. From the houses and alleys came a chorus of weeping and post-viral coughs.

It was very, very different from the sounds Aktus had been told to expect in Hedonia, which were supposed to amount to nothing less than an ever-flowing symphony of carnal delight, made up of bedposts creaking, voices moaning, and the overlapping slapping of body parts.

Some of his comrades had wanted to abandon the city at once. But Aktus was stubborn. He'd come all this way, and wasn't ready to give up on his quest to drain his balls in a Hedonian brothel. So they'd split up to search for an oasis of pleasure in this ill-fated plague-pit.

Perhaps that was one just ahead of him?

He stopped outside a building lit by a single red lantern. The place was called The Quimcushion, and had a picture on the sign of a pillow that looked like a pussy getting stabbed at by dozens of needles. The graphic didn't exactly appeal to Aktus' appetites, but the buildings on either side – the Red Thread and the Wolf Den, respectively – were both locked and shuttered. So he ascended the steps, only to be blocked at the entrance by the doorman, an oafish looking chap with cauliflower ears and a row of replacement wooden teeth.

"Sorry mate," said the bouncer, "all full tonight."

Aktus glared at the man. Were they really full up, or did the doorman just not like the look of him?

It wasn't hard to imagine why. Like the rest of his comrades in the Axes of Aarseth, Aktus cultivated a particular appearance. His hair was long and smeared with black dye that made it appear wet, thick, and bedraggled. The inchoate image of a skull had been painted on his face with black and white make-up, giving him the aspect of some leering sort of ghost. It was an image designed to bring terror to the foes of the Axes, and they wore it both on and off the battlefield, hoping the style would one day be considered iconic.

"Oh shit!" people would say. "There go the Axes of Aarseth!"

Thus men would flee, and women would moisten, at the thought of the mercenaries' might. As it was, however, few in this region had even heard of the Axes, often taking them for weirdos, dressed up, perhaps, for some fancy-dress gathering. Nonetheless, Aktus didn't like getting discriminated against because of his appearance. It made him want to poke those judgemental eyes with his thumbs until the juice came out like jelly. He thought about doing just that to the bouncer right now – it'd be easy enough.

Then he changed his mind. Perhaps the man wasn't keeping him out because of the makeup he wore. Maybe the place really was full? Most of the brothels were shut or boarded up, after all.

He growled his displeasure and departed, passing block after block of more boarded-up bordellos. Finally, his vision alighted on a wash of brilliant light. A building stood ahead of him, fronted with dozens of lanterns, all of them red. On the sign was a flower with a pussy in the centre. The paint had been lacquered, so the petals and the lips looked perpetually wet. A sign on the wall read:

The Unwithering Flower.
Cleanest brothel in all of Hedonia

> Our girls do it all, no question, no complaint
> Reasonable rates, all guests welcome!

Aktus shrugged and stepped inside. The place smelled of cheap paint and sawdust, as though it'd recently been refurbished. Behind the desk in the foyer sat a man with a swarthy complexion, a turban, and a luscious black beard tapering to a point. Being well-travelled, Aktus recognised him as a native of Alhazred, where tongues of rainbow fire go dancing with the desert siroccos after dusk.

"Hello and welcome, my friend!" the man said with a smile on his face. "I am Narseh. I take it you're ready to experience the pleasures of The Unwithering Flower, home to the cleanest, most obedient whores in all of Hedonia?"

"Reckon I am," said Aktus.

"Excellent! You'll have to pay upfront, of course."

Aktus' eyes went wide as Narseh listed the price.

"The sign said the rates were reasonable," he protested.

"Oh but they are! Haven't you noticed there's been a bit of a plague? Sadly, the whores of Hedonia have been decimated, which means it's very much a seller's market right now. But don't think I'm trying to swindle you. Just wait till you get a load of our girls! They'll do anything you want them to, anything at all – just say it, and they'll do it, they won't even blink. You'll think they've got no will of their own!" Narseh paused, and cleared his throat. "Assuming you want a girl, of course. We've got boys here as well, even a hermaphrodite. We're thinking of bringing in a jaguar, for the more jaded clientele…"

"A girl will be fine," said Aktus.

"Great!" said Narseh, and held out an expectant hand.

Aktus reached into his moneybag for a fistful of silver. Narseh counted the coins, squirrelled them away in his robes, then smiled once again.

"Please follow me," he said. Pausing, he glanced at the massive, two-headed axe slung across Aktus' back, its blades barely concealed by a thick leather sheath. "Perhaps you'd like to stow your weapon in the lobby?"

"Never!" said Aktus. "The Axes of Aarseth never hand over our weapons!"

"Good for you, I suppose. Just don't go chopping up the girls, or I'll have to charge you extra. Okay?"

Aktus nodded, not quite sure if the man was joking or not.

Narseh led him down a hallway and into a room, where he told him to wait.

"She'll be along shortly," he said. "If you don't like the look of her, let me know, and I'll fetch you another."

Aktus nodded again and Narseh disappeared, leaving him alone. He paced the room, examining the décor. In the centre was a bed with crimson covers. On the walls, frescoes of sex acts stretched from floor to ceiling, creating a kaleidoscope of coitus, cunnilingus and fellatio, with images of dripping pink pussy lips and arcs of spurting jism providing a border.

With the images getting him right in the mood, he utterly failed to notice the macabre hieroglyphs cunningly obscured by the lurid façade. Images of entrails, buzzards, and twisted skeletons hid amongst explosions of cum, tufts of pubic hair, even labial folds. Anyone would have had a hard time detecting them, let alone someone whose blood was rushing southwards, as Aktus' presently was.

He stripped off and waited with a throbbing erection. Soon,

the door opened and a woman walked in, wearing a rose-coloured robe.

Aktus awaited her fearful response. After all, he was six-foot-four, with a body striped with scars and a face caked with ghastly corpse-paint. Instead, she just smiled at him, fastened the door in her wake, and threw off her robe. His eyes opened wide as he beheld her naked body. She was nubile, and pale, with luscious dark hair.

Her perky breasts bounced as she strode to him and dropped to her knees. She started sucking immediately, making hungry, moaning sounds, as though she were partaking of some unearthly delight, rather than a mercenary's unwashed cock. She took him in deeper and deeper, as far as he could go.

Her gag reflex must be totally dead! he thought.

The hungry, moaning sounds continued as she impaled her oesophagus over and over on his prick, until Aktus was shuddering and spurting and clutching her head in his hands.

She got up, licked her lips, then took hold of his prick and led him to the bed, where she nursed him to hardness again. Then she lay there, like a doll, waiting to be posed. He spread her legs and thrust himself inside, finding her gripping and wet. She made yet more hungry, moaning sounds, shuddering as if from a series of orgasms.

Had Aktus been a more attentive lover, he would've realised she was faking it, that her sighs were like a soundtrack on repeat, her spasms of pleasure nothing but a pantomime. He might've even seen that there was something very strange, even something very *wrong* about her. But he neither noticed, nor cared. He was too busy climbing a mountain of pleasure – and exploding all over the summit.

He fell back on the bed in the aftermath of orgasm. She lay in his arms, almost utterly still. Her body smelt strongly of flowers. The scent was in her hair, her skin, even in the juice from her pussy and the spittle from her mouth. The odour struck him as a little peculiar, but he didn't really question it. Instead he considered how much time he had left, and how much more he could do to her before it ran out. Would he be able to go up the back passage, he wondered?

She'll probably refuse, or ask for more money, he thought, but when he broached the subject she merely bent over and spread her cheeks wide.

He slid inside. Her arsehole was lubricated, too, as if she'd been prepared for this. It was also immaculately clean, as if she'd been scrubbed from the inside. After he came again, he lay there, too exhausted by his triple performance to go another round. Still, she knelt beside him, sucking on his now-flaccid member, in spite of the places it'd been, till a knock rattled the door.

"Closing time!" called Narseh's voice.

The woman sprang up immediately and put on her robe. At the door, she turned back and smiled, then departed. Only then did it occur to Aktus that, in spite of all her moaning, she hadn't said a word.

***

Another satisfied customer! Narseh thought as he hustled the mercenary out into the street. The man looked weak in the knees, dazed with post-coital ecstasy.

Once he'd shut the door and bolted it, he descended into

the depths of The Unwithering Flower, to a secret chamber where his prostitutes were gathering. One by one, they settled their bodies onto the benches that dotted the chamber like funeral slabs.

As was quite fitting. They were all dead, of course.

Chapter 4: Closing Time

Narseh inspected his resting stable of hoes. In the dim light, they looked very dead indeed. Only the magick of the hieroglyphs, hidden in the frescoes on the walls, gave them their semblance of life. Narseh wasn't entirely sure how it worked, but somehow the hieroglyphs cast a spell to deceive the eyes of the unwitting patrons. Of course, their other senses had to be fooled as well.

The girls had to *feel* alive, for one thing, not just look it. Luckily, Wena had been able to arrest their decay with some other sort of spell, which stopped them from bloating or falling to pieces. A third spell lent warmth to their otherwise cold, clammy flesh.

Since they still smelt like death, and lacked a means of self-lubrication, further solutions were required. Removing and replacing their internal organs with a mixture of sawdust and flowers gave them a floral scent, like those of Wena's servants. Before each session with a client, aromatic oils were applied liberally to their various orifices.

As for their sexual performances, Narseh had no clue – that was all Wena's doing. Somehow she'd programmed their bodies with a rote set of acts, the same way her butlers were programmed to heave around her luggage or stand guard at her door.

Narseh clapped his hands. "Chop, chop!" he called. "Let's get this show on the road!"

His former galley slaves hurried into the room. They'd been

given new jobs as brothel attendants. Or perhaps they were mortuary workers? He supposed there wasn't really a word for what they did. This venture of theirs seemed utterly unprecedented. What did that make him, he wondered – a pimp, a mortician, or a grave-robber? A pimptician? A necro-panderer? It really didn't matter. What mattered was the coin clinking into his coffers – which it was.

The business itself had been easy enough to set up. With hundreds of buildings left vacant in the wake of the plague, no one had questioned when they'd simply moved in to one, Narseh acting as if he owned the place. As for his stable of strumpets, he'd snatched them up at a steal. Some of them he'd literally stolen, looting the plague pits by night for the sexiest corpses. Others he'd purchased for a pittance from madams and pimps who'd been only too happy to turn a final profit, however meagre, from the bodies of their whores.

He watched as his minions went to work on the cadavers, douching out their pussies and arseholes, then scrubbing them with sponges on sticks. Narseh's mouth wrinkled with disgust. All that goo sluicing out. He was glad he had slaves for this sort of work!

Even harder to clean was the cum accrued from the performance of fellatio. It dribbled down their throats and seeped into the sawdust stuffing that filled their torsos. The only way to deal with the mess was to open them up and scoop out the soiled bits directly. The zombified whores had to be so treated every other day, or the smell would seep out and arouse the suspicions of the patrons. Narseh had thought about banning fellatio to save all that hassle, but what sort of brothel worth its salt would ever do that? He'd be the laughing stock of Hedonia if he dared take the mouth off the menu!

His slaves busily undid the sutures on the bodies of the girls, scooped the soiled stuffing from within, dumped it in a bin, and replaced it with fresh batches of sawdust and roses.

"Watch it, moron!" snapped Narseh, as one added way too many petals to the mixture. "Those are expensive. Use more sawdust, or I'll dock your pay!"

"But you don't pay me, boss."

"And I never will. Not with that attitude!" He strode away, grumbling to himself. But it was all for show, of course. The cost of the flowers was nothing compared to how much money he was making overall.

The plague had killed off over a third of the city's population. Many of the brothels were still closed or running at less than half capacity, even as the customers began to trickle back in from abroad, creating a surfeit of demand the beleaguered bordellos couldn't meet. So, in steps Narseh to the rescue, with his stable of ravishing beauties – provided one saw them in the optimal light.

It was the perfect setup. Squatting in the building, they therefore paid no rent; their employees were dead, and needed no wages or food. The only real expense was that blasted twenty-percent prostitution tax. But since Narseh grossly underdeclared all his profits, even the taxman wasn't much of a problem.

He grinned from ear-to-ear as he stepped into the necromancer's chamber – which, given recent developments, was his chamber, too.

"Hello my sweet," he said, beaming with happiness.

Wena lay on the mat, not passed out, but clearly exhausted.

Her two undead butlers stood like statues by the door. The rest of the zombies from her galley had been hidden in the hollows of the brothel's walls, entombed but ever vigilant, just waiting for their mistress' command. Narseh liked to think of them as bouncers on call. They'd certainly be handy, should trouble arise.

She murmured a greeting, still lying prone on the floor.

"You know it's a shame we can't stay open longer," said Narseh, as he transferred coins from his pockets to the over-flowing treasure chest in the corner. "We'd make even more money!"

"I need to rest," said Wena. "Maintaining all those spells is exhausting."

"Of course it is, my sweet," said Narseh. "And you certainly deserve some downtime. Here, let me help you into bed."

He knelt beside her. For a moment her zombie butlers tensed, as they always did, alert to any possible threat to their mistress. She pacified them both with a glance as Narseh picked her up and carried her over to the bed. She felt light in his arms. It seemed she'd lost weight since the brothel had opened just a few months ago. He supposed it must be tiring work indeed that she was doing, meditating ten hours a day to keep all the spells running smoothly. Still, he wished she didn't need quite so much rest. It was cutting into their profits!

He laid her on the bed and sat beside her, stroking her face.

"You have a rest now, my sweet," he said. "We've got an-other full day ahead of us tomorrow. I'm off to do some ac-counting…"

As he made a move to rise, she held him by the wrist. "Don't go," she said, a look of languid lust in her eyes. She guided his hand down to the warmth between her thighs.

"I thought you needed a break?" he said. "You should probably avoid too much strenuous activity…"

"I need *this*," she said. "I want this. The magick, it's not just physically exhausting, it's mentally draining, as well. I need some brightness. I need some life! So do you, you know. You can't just think about profits all day."

The fuck I can't, thought Narseh.

"Come on," she said.

She drew up her dress and pressed his hand firmly against her. She was hot and wet. He bathed his fingers in the moisture, teasing her gently. She gave a relaxed sigh and started squirming her body on the bed, slowly getting hotter and wetter, until she pushed his hand away, primed for something deeper.

"Get undressed," she said. "Let me see you."

Narseh stood up and began to disrobe.

***

Once again, as Wena lay watching him, she found herself wondering why she was so attracted to this man. His looks certainly provided part of the answer. His naked body was handsome and lean in the light of the lanterns. He took off his turban, letting his long, dark hair fall down past his shoulders.

What else did she admire? His silver tongue, perhaps. He always seemed to know just the right thing to say, and could read other people in ways that she couldn't. After all, she'd spent her youth being trained as a necromancer, taught to deal with the dead things, not the living. He, on the other hand, was worldly, well-travelled. His way with people fascinated her, and his charisma was undeniable.

His greed, though... sometimes she wondered if there was anything in him other than a love for accumulating money. Was he falling for her, as she was for him – or was he merely managing another investment?

Or maybe I'm just desperate, she thought.

After all, few people outside of Khem would get in bed with a necromancer. Perhaps loneliness had made her seek out his affection, the way a starving dog might fawn upon the lousiest of masters for a meagre scrap of food. For a moment, as he stood silhouetted before the lantern, his face transformed into a mask of black shadow, she saw only the darkness in their union.

Then he climbed upon the bed and smiled in the light. Wena melted. Surely there was true love and brightness inside of him. Surely he was loving her, too – not just with his body, but his soul?

In spite of her exhaustion she jumped into his arms, casting off her dress and fondling his prick as they kissed. She tried to mount him in the lotus position, so she could look into his eyes and kiss him on the lips as they fucked, but he gently disentangled their legs and coaxed her up on all fours. She let him, being rather fond of doggy-style, too.

Reaching back, she guided him inside of her, murmuring softly as he entered. Narseh knelt behind her, his hands on her hips, building up a gentle momentum. She glanced over her shoulder at him with lusty eyes, seeking to fire his own passion even brighter. He met her gaze eagerly and pumped harder, making her quiver. Then her face turned away as she let out a series of almost-silent moans.

***

Appealing though the sight was of Wena's slim, dusky body stretched out before him, tapering away from her rump, Narseh looked past her to the treasure chest in the corner. The sight of gold and riches always made him hornier. That's why he'd chosen this sexual position – he wanted to stare at his burgeoning wealth as they went at it.

He could see his own reflection in the gemstones littering the horde, and in the contours of a statue atop the lot. It depicted a naked and beautiful courtesan. Just a moulded image, of course, which couldn't compare to the flesh-and-blood woman trembling on his prick. And yet, as their rutting wore on, he found himself spending more time looking at the statue than at Wena, taking in its gleaming thighs, its jewel-tipped breasts, the reflection of the firelight dancing across its sleek, gilded surface like mercury. In his preoccupation, he almost didn't notice when Wena succumbed to a shuddering orgasm.

He felt her get wetter and wider around him. Glancing down between the peachy round cheeks of her butt, he saw her cute arsehole twitching from spasms of pleasure. Her whole body quivered and shook. Satisfied that she was satisfied, he launched a crescendo of thrusts that had her shuddering again before he spurted inside of her. The orgasm deadened his vision, as it so often did, dimming every sense except that which resided in his prick. Still he kept sight of the horde, even as the rest of the room dimmed into darkness, so that the gemstones, and the coins, and the gold figurine hung like luminescent ghosts in the void of his climax.

He slowed to a stop. Wena slipped off his prick and rolled

over onto her back. She smiled and wriggled with residual delight.

She really is getting thin, he thought, spying the outlines of her ribs against her skin.

Then his eyes were drawn to her pussy, where cum dribbled out in a white rivulet.

"You're sure you won't get pregnant?" he asked.

***

She shot him an irritated look; he'd soured her mood. "You ask that every time," she snapped.

"It's just that a pregnancy might distract from our work…"

"And I told you not to worry about it. Okay?"

"Fine, fine," he said, stretching out beside her, though she suspected he still wasn't entirely mollified.

Wena sighed. As a necromancer, unwanted pregnancies were rarely a concern. Many of her counterparts in Khem couldn't even conceive; their bodies were too heavily infused with the energies of death. Those who could often brought forth abominations, grave-born things that were half-living, half-dead. Since Wena had been banished before her training was complete, her womb wasn't yet thoroughly steeped; she could still conceive normally – if she wanted to. It was entirely her choice. She had enough magickal awareness to recognise the moment of conception, and enough necromantic power to abort any offspring at once, should that be her will.

And should her magick somehow fail to do the job, the city of Hedonia was a hub of abortionists and apothecaries who'd be only too willing to help. Thousands of unwanted foetuses were snuffed every day, flushed down the drains or tossed into the streets to provide the wild dogs with a ready source of protein. There must have been millions of them, she thought, floating like tadpoles in the sewers below. If she reached out with her Death Sight she might sense them all swarming there, an ocean of accumulated anti-birth.

But she didn't want to sense them. This whole change of topic was making her upset, plunging her thoughts into darkness.

"How long are we going to keep doing this?" she asked.

"As long as you want me too, my sweet," said Narseh with a randy-looking smile.

"Not the sex, silly. This business."

"As long as we can get away with it."

"I'm serious, Narseh. We can't go on like this forever. The longer we continue, the more chance there is someone will notice the hieroglyphs, or see through the magick. Anyone with second sight who happens by would figure out the truth straightaway. If the frescoes are damaged – even if the *paint* starts to peel – then the spells will be compromised. If people figure out they've been having sex with corpses, we'll be lynched from the nearest fucking lamppost!"

"We'll be fine. I have the frescoes checked for damage every day. And if anyone does figure out the truth, I'll just bribe them to be silent. Money talks, remember?"

"It's not just the difficulty in maintaining the illusions," she said. 'The longer I sustain a spell of this magnitude, the more deathly energies will build up. In the walls, in the soil, in the very air. The miasma's getting thick as it is. So much necromantic power can have horrible side effects, and I wasn't really taught how to handle them. I got kicked out before I could finish that part of my training…"

"You worry too much, my love," he said. "You're just getting gloomy from exhaustion. Sleep, rest, and tomorrow you'll feel better." He stretched out a blanket to cover her body, then leaned in and kissed her on the mouth. "I'll be back soon," he said. "I just have to go balance the ledger."

For a moment, she clung to his warmth, then let him slip away into the shadows. But, unable to sleep, she tossed and turned beneath the covers. She couldn't shake the feeling that something was about to go very, very wrong.

Chapter 5: Boys Night Out

Aktus was in the hotel bar, nursing a pint of black lager, when two of his comrades emerged from their quarters and came shambling to his table, sitting down with a grumble. Even through their corpse-paint he could tell they were hungover. They propped their axes against the wall and ordered up drinks. The fearful bar staff jumped to attention, while the rest of the patrons gave the mercenaries a wide-berth, wary of their sinister makeup and their ever-present axes.

"Where're the others?" Aktus asked as the drinks arrived and the two sat there swigging.

Their company totalled ten, a pretty meagre sum by the standards of mercenary bands, which often had hundreds or thousands of members. Still, what the Axes of Aarseth lacked in numbers they made up for in might. Each was as deadly as a full score of lesser soldiers, and commanded an income to match. On account of this, they were called the 'Twennies,' or 'Twenty-men.' Their massive axes were too heavy for most others to even pick up, let alone wield. Mastering those weapons had taken them years of harsh training, until their arms had grown thick as some men's thighs, and their bodies were towers of muscle and strength. They cut through ranks of infantry like sickles through wheat.

"Still in bed," said Immo, the largest of the group, not just in muscle but in fat. His face, though streaked with corpse-paint, seemed jolly nonetheless. He laughed as he continued. "They all struck out last night. Got so frustrated with blue balls they came back here and drank till they dropped. I doubt they'll be up for a couple more hours!"

"How did you do?" asked Aktus.

"Not so great. Wandered around for a while, then finally managed to find myself a shrivelled old whore. She said she'd been the best in Hedonia, back in her day, though you sure couldn't tell that by looking at her now. A real double-bagger, that's for sure. She even brought her own bags! One for me, another for her. We must've looked like two condemned criminals, having a tryst before our date with the hangman. Still, the blowjob was good. Her wooden teeth came right out of her mouth!"

Gorgo, the third of their number and the tallest, made a sickened sound and spat a mouthful of lager on the floor. His features were gaunt. Rings of black paint made his eyes look almost skeletally sunken.

"What about you?" asked Aktus, turning towards him.

"Not so great either. I ended up having to settle for a lady-boy."

Immo laughed. "Are you sure you '*settled*?' Maybe that's just what you were after all along!"

"Fuck you," said Gorgo.

"Oh, don't be like that. Nothing wrong with ladyboys. Let's face it, even when you're with a girl, you only end up trying to fuck them up the arse anyway. At least with a tranny you know what's on the menu! Saves a lot of beating around the bush, so to speak."

"Is that what you did with this vintage old sexpot of yours?"

"I certainly tried, but the years hadn't been kind to her down there. Too many sessions of anal gymnastics left her full-prolapse. It was like trying to throat-fuck a snake."

Gorgo groaned and looked nauseous, not just from his hangover. "You're disgusting," he said, but Immo just laughed. Gorgo turned to Aktus instead. "How about you?"

Aktus beamed, then regaled them with a tale of the pleasures he'd experienced at The Unwithering Flower. Immo and Gorgo hung on his words as he gave them a blow-by-blow description of the blowjob he'd received, followed by the rest of his sexcapades. By the time he'd finished they looked a lot less hungover, and a great deal more animated.

"I guess we know where we're going tonight!" said Immo with a broad grin.

***

It was, indeed, several hours before the rest of their company put in an appearance. By then, having been steadily drinking while they waited, Aktus was drunk, Gorgo was wasted, and Immo well on the way to soused.

The others put in a good effort to catch up, and before long they stumbled together down the Hedonian streets, bumping into strangers, roaring, singing, laughing in the lantern-lit dusk. Aktus had to struggle to find his way back to the Unwithering Flower, his friends mocking him, saying he must've passed out and imagined the whole thing, that he'd probably had sex with a hobo in a state of delirium. He was just about to throw a punch when he saw the tell-tale glow of a dozen red lanterns and the image of a flower with a pussy in the middle.

"There!" he said.

They hustled to the doors, then Immo stopped them with

a slurred warning.

"Gotta compozhe ourshelves," he said, staggering to keep his balance. "Don't wanta sheem too pishted, or they won't lettusssh in. Shavvy?"

Agreeing, they all took a moment, straightening their backs and sucking down sobering breaths.

With the dream-like confidence of someone very drunk, Aktus felt – nay, he *knew* – that he could clear his head and reverse the effects of the alcohol with nothing but pure, un-mitigated willpower. He focused his mind. Suddenly the world seemed brighter, sharper, his vision more focused. His body felt steady, as sober as could be. He took a step –

And reeled right into Immo, who laughed. "Fuck it," he said. "Letsh go in."

***

The doors opened, and in blundered a whole host of drunk, dangerous, heavily armed men. Narseh took a wary look at them, then saw their moneybags were bulging!

He smiled widely and spoke to the one he recognised. "Hel-lo again, my friend! I see you've come back to sup some more nectar from the Flower! And brought company!"

"I sure have," said Aktus, swaying on his feet. "Do we get a group discount?"

Narseh chuckled. "No discounts, I'm afraid. But I'm sure your joy will be doubled by the presence of your comrades."

One of the mercenaries pushed forth from the back of the ranks.

"Are you shaying we're gonna fuck each other?" he growled.

"Of course not," said Narseh. "I merely meant that it will be a comradely exercise for you, since you're all here together. Yes?"

The mercenary glared suspiciously at him a moment longer, then shrugged, his drunken anger seemingly diffused.

"Coins on the counter, gentlemen," said Narseh.

They reached into their moneybags and started slamming down silver. Some were so drunk they gave him too much, which he pocketed regardless. Others had miscounted and given too little; from them he demanded the remainder, and pocketed that, as well.

"I take it you'll be keeping your weapons with you?" he asked, remembering Aktus' habit from the previous evening.

"Where we go, they go," one of them said.

"As you please. Follow me."

Narseh led them through the halls, showing each to a room. Before long, he was alone in the corridor – or so he thought, until a hand reached out from the darkness, grabbing his shoulder with terrifying strength.

Chapter 6: Half-Mast

He whirled. Behind him stood one of Wena's undead butlers, clutching his shoulder with the ignorant strength of the dead.

"Get off me, you oaf!" he ordered, attempting to brush off its grip.

But the implacable corpse was too strong. It all but dragged him down the corridor and into Wena's chamber. Only then did it let go.

Upset at being manhandled, Narseh kicked the unfeeling zombie in the shin, then glanced down at Wena, who sat in a circle of incense sticks in the centre of the room. He knew from her look of intense concentration she was busy meditating, maintaining the spells. Her beautiful face was beaded with sweat from the effort.

"What do you think you're doing?" he snapped, gesturing towards her undead servant. "We can't have those *things* out there wandering the halls! What if someone saw them?"

"I don't like the look of those mercenaries," she said, without looking up at him.

"I'll admit that their makeup is a little peculiar –"

"It's not the makeup I'm worried about, Narseh. They're drunk, dangerous."

"I'd say far more of the former than the latter. Those boys are plastered! They're too drunk to know where they are, let alone figure out what's going on."

"I hope you're right."

"Of course I am. As I've told you, you worry too much, my

dear."

He bent to kiss her on the cheek, then went to empty his pocketfuls of coins into the treasure chest. His heart grew more buoyant with every single CLINK!

***

Immo fell across the bed after failing a titanic struggle to remove his own trousers. Finally, he managed to wrestle them off, and lay there with his senses spinning. The room's decorative frescoes whirled before his eyes, creating a kaleidoscope of lips, hips, and thighs. Within the blur were hints of hieroglyphs he couldn't quite see, sinister images of buzzards and skulls.

He ignored them and played with his prick instead, finding it limp and unresponsive from the gallons of lager he'd imbibed.

Poor girl's really gonna have her work cut out for her, he mused.

Just then, the door opened and a woman stepped in. He tried to make out her features, but the world kept billowing before his eyes like a curtain in the breeze. With an effort of will he got it to stay still long enough to see that she was pretty and pale.

No bags needed this time, he thought with a smile.

She slipped off her robe and strode over to the bed, smelling of roses. At once, she went to work between his legs, sucking his flaccid little cock into her mouth and stroking it nimbly with her fingers. It stayed limp for a while, then grew semierect, so that it hung between her lips like a piece of pale rope. Still she kept sucking it, coaxing it, stroking it. Her eyes looked hungry as they stared into his, bloated with a likeness of lust. She moaned as if tasting a delicacy, as though his half-awake snake were giving her some kind of blazing oral orgasm.

Is she mocking me? Immo wondered, feeling his jovial persona begin to unravel.

Any other woman would've given up by now, and told him to forget it. "These things happen," she would've said, shrugging. "Sober up and come back later." But this one kept plying his limpness as though it were the stiffest, most fabulous cock in the world.

Of course, it didn't occur to him that this was all just a rote, pre-programmed display; he read mockery in those blank, soulless eyes. She was laughing at him inwardly, he was sure, acting as though he were a stud when he couldn't get it up. This was a whole new species of ridicule!

"Get offa me!" he shouted, pushing her from the bed.

She fell to the floor. For a moment she knelt there, looking blank. Then she started playing with herself, teasing her nipples and fingering her lubricated pussy. She started moaning wantonly, as if trying to arouse him, as if oblivious to the anger in his eyes.

Fucking bitch is still taunting me! he thought.

Immo got to his feet, swaying as he did. He reeled, and saw the walls reeling with him. The frescoes' images swirled all around, mocking him in turn with their depictions of coitus and fellatio, of penetrated pussies and steel-rod erections.

"FUCK!" he roared.

He groped for his axe and swung its leather-sheathed head at the wall. Whether deliberately or not, he managed to smash the blade straight thought the centre of a pussy, shattering the flimsy plaster and destroying the hieroglyphs hidden amid the labia.

The room suddenly seemed darker. The scent of flowers was joined by a whiff of decay. Immo knew that smell from the battlefield. It stirred up a surge of adrenaline, clearing away his vertigo and focusing his mind through its alcoholic haze.

It came from the girl, who still knelt on the floor, fingering her pussy and plucking her nipples. Between her breasts was a suture he was sure hadn't been there before. It ran to her navel, as though her body had been opened up and sewn back together. Her skin was not only pale, it was bloodless, and grey.

When she looked up at him, her unfeeling eyes were made of glass.

Immo let out a horrified yell and started pulling at the leather sheathing his axe's broad blades.

Chapter 7: Stiffs

"We've got a breach," said Wena. "One of those idiots just smashed up a fresco!"

"How's he reacting?" asked Narseh. "Can we bribe him?"

Closing her own eyes, she looked through those of the dead girl. She saw Immo standing before her, naked and enraged, stripping the sheath from his axe.

"I think he wants payment in blood!" she said.

"Then we'll have to drain *his* coffers of it first," said Narseh. "Deal with him!"

Wena sent her full consciousness into the corpse. She felt its cold flesh all around her as though it were her own. She even felt the cum-soaked sawdust filling its chest.

She forced the dead meat to its feet and stood facing the mercenary, just as he whipped off the leather and laid bare the gleaming blade. He swung. Wena ducked her dead puppet beneath the blur of blue steel and rushed him, grabbing his balls in one hand and his throat in the other. She squeezed with undead might until his trachea snapped and his testicles burst between her surrogate fingers.

The effort left her drained, not to mention distracted. For a dizzying moment she lost all control of her spells. Throughout the halls and the rooms of The Unwithering Flower, the magickal light flickered and dimmed, allowing naked death to peek out from the gloom.

***

Aktus was ploughing his whore from behind when he first heard the distant cries. He thought briefly about investigating, but the sounds had been muffled by the walls, were probably cries of pleasure anyway, and his own pleasure was far too imminent.

So, he kept pumping, until the light in the room faded like a guttering candle and his whore's floral scent became mingled with rot. Her moans fell silent. Her skin went pallid and dry.

Fuck! he thought, pulling out of her suddenly cooled pussy and scrambling to the back of the bed.

She turned and looked at him with a slack, dead face. As the lights shimmered again, her lips curved in a glistening smile, and she began crawling across the covers towards him.

***

"Oh fuck!" Wena gasped, her eyes popping open. "Oh fuck, oh fuck. I lost it, Narseh. I lost it!"

"Lost what?"

"Control of the spell. Just for a few seconds. But they would've seen everything!"

A series of horrified shouts rose up from the brothel, confirming her fears.

"We need to contain it," said Narseh. "It's time to clean house. Understand?"

Wena nodded grimly, and shut her eyes again.

***

Gorgo lay on the bed in blissful ignorance, eyes closed so he could focus on the blowjob he was getting.

His eyes had been closed for a while. Consequently, he hadn't seen the light grow dim, nor had he seen the cadaverous face of the creature sucking his cock. He hadn't heard the shouts and the screams of his comrades, either, for his room shared a wall with a noisy pub next door.

Thus he lay in blissful ignorance, marvelling at the skills of his fellator. She was taking him deeply, right to the root. There was no touch of teeth –

-- until now.

The teeth bit down savagely, shearing him off. He screamed, eyes open now, seeing the blood from his stump blasting across a face that looked utterly dead. He'd wanted to give her a facial, of course – just not like this!

He saw the ragged remnants of his member protruding between her desiccated lips. Then he passed out from shock and started bleeding to death.

***

Aktus stared in confusion at the smiling girl crawling toward him. She wasn't moaning anymore, wasn't making any noises at all.

Was this all some weird hallucination, he wondered? Had someone spiked one of his drinks with psychedelics? His fellow Axes were fond of such pranks ...

But the stench had been so real! He still felt it clinging to his nostrils! And what about the shouts he'd heard from down the hall? What about the other red flags, like the weird muteness of the women, and their peculiar emotionlessness? Something was definitely wrong here!

From her crawling crouch, the woman suddenly sprang towards him with jaws open wide. He threw himself sideways off the bed, letting her land on the pillows behind him. Scrambling to his feet, he dashed across the room, just as she took another lunge. She missed him by a hair and crashed against the wall. The light had begun to flicker and strobe, making her look beautiful one moment, cadaverous the next. Her sultry smile appeared and disappeared with the coming and going of the light, like a face in a frenzied game of peek-a-boo.

She leapt at him.

"Fuck!" he shouted.

His axe sat propped against the wall. He picked it up, and without having time to whip off the sheath, struck her in the head, hoping that bludgeoning force would be enough to do the job.

The blade hit her hard, sending her reeling. One of her eyes popped out and rolled across the floor. As the light flickered low again he saw that it was made of cut glass. The skull behind the hollow socket was totally empty.

"Fuck!" he roared again.

She rushed towards him in a frenzy, grasping at the axe. The sheath was still on it. For a moment they wrestled with the weapon between them. Then the sheath tore loose, and the dead girl stumbled backwards, holding it. She bit and clawed at it fiercely, as though she were rending human flesh.

Aktus gaped in horror. In her sickening state of undeath, she had lost the ability to differentiate people from objects. Then he swung the naked blade and took her apart at the middle.

As the light shone bright, she seemed to die just like anyone else, collapsing to the ground in a welter of blood. Then the light guttered down again, revealing a bloodless cadaver, from which sodden bits of sawdust and petals spilled out, like a mulch of autumn leaves, soaked not with rain but with semen.

The scent of stale cum joined the reek of decay. Aktus tried not to vomit. He heard the screams rising up anew all around him – the screams of his comrades, the Axes of Aarseth!

"I'm coming, brothers!" he shouted, running to the door.

It was locked.

More freakish sorcery! he thought.

He knew, in spite of his drunkenness, fear, and adrenaline, that the vilest of magick was at work in this brothel. Into his mind flashed an image of the man from Alhazred.

"You bastard," he growled. "I'll fix you!"

He cleaved and chopped through the door and forced his way into the hall, into yet more flickering light and the perfume of roses tainted with the odour of death.

Another door exploded into rubble and Sadek, one of Aktus' companions, fell sprawling with a dead woman clinging to his back. His eyes had been ripped from their sockets, and the woman was gnawing at the side of his neck, bathing herself in a gush of arterial blood.

"Bitch!" shouted Aktus, shearing off her head with a single blow.

She kept moving regardless, mauling Sadek with her hands in lieu of her mouth. Since his friend was already as good as dead anyway, Aktus hacked both of them in half. Dismembered, the woman grew finally still, spilling sawdust and roses from her bisected ribs.

Aktus grit his teeth. His brothers were dying!

Though, by the sounds, some were still alive. He could hear them fighting to survive. He rushed to the closest room and swung his axe at the door. It bit through wood, then flesh, then bone. The blade came back bloody, and a body hit the floor.

Aktus stared in horror through the splintered ruins. One of his bros had been backed up against the door, struggling with a dead thing; now he was a dead thing himself, cleft through the spine by Aktus' own unwitting axe.

"Fuck!" shouted Aktus, and then a prostitute zombie crashed through the wrecked door, trampling the body of his comrade underfoot.

He split her down the middle, from forehead to groin. She collapsed with a predictable outpouring of potpourri, sawdust, and jism.

Aktus rushed for the next room, from which came yet more shouting.

Better use my shoulder this time! he thought, having learned a cruel lesson from the accidental butchering of his comrade.

He stepped back and got ready to shoulder-charge the door, but before he could, a figure burst from the wall behind him, reeking of death and wrapped in bright saffron.

Chapter 8: Frenzy

"How's it going out there?" asked Narseh as he paced about the room.

"Badly," said Wena. "These guys are tough. I've got five of them down, but the rest are still going. They've already killed a dozen of the girls!"

"*Killed?* How can they be killed? They're already dead!"

"Destroyed, then. The magick is broken by bodily dismemberment. I can't animate corpses if they're in a dozen pieces! Narseh, we need to go, *now*. Even if we manage to kill everyone here, people will come looking for them. Then there's the screaming –"

"You're overreacting," he said. "I'm sure it's not as bad as you say. Why don't I take a peek for myself?"

"Narseh, no!" she shouted. "Don't go out there!"

But he'd already hurried from the room.

***

The creature in saffron silks cinched its arms around Aktus' chest before he had time to react. It bit at his neck, but its teeth had rotted out long ago, leaving only mummified gums that grasped at the flesh without breaking the skin.

The real danger came from its arms. They squeezed like a vice, cracking one of his ribs. If he didn't act fast, he'd be crushed! He still had his axe, but his upper arms being pinned against his sides prevented him from swinging it. He dropped the useless weapon and grabbed the creature's wrists. They were withered and wrapped, like those of a mummy, but coursing with the pitiless power of a solid steel trap. Aktus knew he had only one chance – to throw all of his strength into one last attempt to break free, before it was too late.

He gritted his teeth and pulled with all his might at the mummified hands, trying to loosen their grip. His muscles bulged, the sinews on his neck standing out like straining ropes. He thought he might tear his own body apart with his exertions. Then he felt the undead arms loosen a little. With a growl of wild fury, he bent at the waist and hurled the withered monster off his back. For all its uncanny strength, the thing was surprisingly light. It crashed to the floor and split its skull on the boards. Eyeballs made of lapis lazuli popped from its head and shot across the hall like a pair of rogue marbles.

But it still wasn't finished. It writhed on the ground, trying to right itself. Aktus picked up his axe and started hacking, refusing to stop until the creature was in motionless pieces. Herbs from its hollowed-out insides flew everywhere, making him sneeze.

Another of his comrades shouted in alarm from somewhere up ahead.

"I'm coming!" called Aktus. It was the sort of exclamation commonly heard in a Hedonian brothel, if not in this particular context.

Aktus raced down the corridor, rounded a corner, and found Borgo fighting with more of the things from the walls. One of them had hold of his axe, trying to pull it away; the other drew back its hand for a gut-punch.

"Borgo, watch out!"

His warning came too late. The mummy's fist plunged into Borgo's guts and came out entangled with intestine. Borgo, done for, slumped to the floor, his face going paler than his corpse paint.

"RAAHH!!" Aktus let out a bloodthirsty roar and charged in, swinging.

***

"What're you doing standing around?" Narseh snapped, as he rushed through the mortuary room where his slaves had paused to listen to the terrible sounds coming from the rest of the brothel. "Get back to work!"

The slaves resumed half-heartedly cleaning, while he hurried into the hall. A bloodthirsty cry from around a corner was followed by a series of hacking sounds. Taking a careful peek, he saw one of the mercenaries – the one who'd come twice now to the brothel, and more times inside of it – looming over two dismembered mummies. His naked body was splattered with blood, sawdust, and rose petals. He was panting like an animal, his muscular chest heaving wide with every breath, like a barrel of sinew and bone fit to burst. When he looked up from the slaughter, he locked eyes with Narseh.

Oh shit, Narseh thought.

***

Aktus, fresh from the heights of his murderous frenzy, saw the man from Alhazred peering around the corner. His blood-thirst rekindled. He forgot all about trying to save the rest of his comrades. He had only one urge now – to catch that awful, bastard proprietor of this murderous establishment, and unfurl his bleeding guts like the threads of a tapestry undone. He roared and gave chase as his enemy fled.

***

"Get out of the way!" shouted Narseh, pushing slaves to the side as he ran back into the mortuary room.

He slammed the door and bolted it behind him, then stood a moment fearful and panting, before turning to the slaves with a display of cool command.

"Right," he said. "Time to bow out. Exit, stage left. You lot, ready the boats. You two, stay by this door. If that maniac gets through, hold him off. Don't worry – I'll make a sacrifice to your souls in the afterlife!"

As they scattered to do his bidding, he raced to Wena's chamber, already regretting his generous offer to reward his dead slaves in the underworld. Then again, he hadn't specified just what the sacrifice would be. Perhaps some apples, brought at a discount, just before the closing of the market?

He found her wide-eyed and anxious, waiting for him, one of the room's ornate tapestries torn from the wall, revealing a staircase behind it, which connected to the tunnels that served as their secret escape route. A cold draft issued from the opening, reeking of death.

"You were right," said Narseh. "It's bad out there. Time to gather our takings and close up shop. Get those undead idiots of yours to carry the chest."

Wena nodded, and sighed with relief. She gestured to the

zombies, who picked up the heavy treasure chest.

"Wait!" cried Narseh. "It isn't full! It can hold more!"

Frantic, he dashed around the room, snatching up coins and bits of jewellery and tossing them in. With Wena's help, it was soon overflowing. She made to close the lid, couldn't, and began to haul out the large and bulky golden courtesan statue.

"No!" He stayed her hand. "We'll tie it! Twist the bedsheets into ropes!"

Once the chest was secured, he still didn't head for the exit, but kept gathering up more of his precious treasure. He stuffed coins in his pockets, hung chains around his neck, loaded rings on his fingers and bracelets on his wrists. He even jammed coins into his slippers.

I guess I finally look the part of a pimp! he thought, though he had no time to admire the effect. Instead, he likewise began filling Wena's pockets and adorning her body with as much jewellery as he could.

Then, from the direction of the mortuary room, came the racket of splintering wood and a mercenary's furious bellow.

"Come on!" Wena threw on her putrescent cloak, regarding him with wide, desperate eyes. "We've got to go!"

The zombies were already manoeuvring the heavy chest slowly down the stairs. Narseh glanced around, heartsick with horror as he saw all the wealth still littering the room.

But another loud CRASH! and the terrified screams of his slaves decided him. He seized Wena's outstretched hand, and together they descended into darkness.

***

The two men who stood guard with surgical knives screamed in terror as Aktus chopped through the door and they saw his wrathful face. He was about to cut them down when they threw away their weapons and surrendered.

"We're just slaves!" one of them pleaded.

The other pointed. "The one you want, he went thattaway!"

Aktus barked like a dog and pushed past them both, following the indicated directions. He arrived in a lavish chamber filled with incense and scattered bits of treasure. From a dark opening in the wall came the perfume of death and a cold, biting wind. Rough-hewn stairs led down. Aktus took them without even blinking.

✻✻✻

Narseh peered around. The solitary torch he'd managed to light showed him a wide, circular tunnel, with a path on either side and a waste-water trench flowing down the middle. It wasn't as filthy as he might have imagined, and was in fact the relic of some past civilization whose buildings had long ago been razed to the ground. The present-day inhabitants of Hedonia lived atop the old ruins, and disposed of their waste in cesspits on the outskirts of town. Thus the sewer itself was mostly unused, filled only with what rubbish from the streets the rains had washed down a few antique gutters.

Slovenly barbarians, he thought, shaking his head. There was indoor plumbing aplenty in Alhazred. He even had a bidet back home!

But Alhazred was an orderly, regulated society. It was hard for an entrepreneur like himself to make a fortune there, with so many rules restraining free trade. That's why he'd come to these savage eastern lands in the first place, where chaos created opportunity.

It also created danger, as was most tellingly shown by his present predicament.

He hurried along the tunnel's side walkway, holding Wena's hand. A pity she was so clingy, especially right now. They could each have been lugging a sackful of coins instead of gripping each other's sweaty fingers! Bad enough he also had to be burdened carrying the torch, but they needed to be able to see where they were going.

They arrived at a junction. To the left, the old sewer continued; to the right, a roughly-hewn passage built by smugglers or pirates in ages past led to a small, hidden jetty by the side of a cliff. There, waiting in readiness for an eventuality just such as this, Narseh's own galley was docked, right beside Wena's.

All they had to do was reach their boats, and they could sail out to sea, leaving their murderous pursuer behind them.

They hurried along the passage, shivering as they went. Overflowing waste-water from the sewer trickled ahead of them, following a gutter worn into the stone floor. Some manner of wet, stinking residue resembling liquefied flesh clung to the walls. The air grew steadily colder, reeking of decay. It seemed as if the very earth itself were a corpse, its bowels rotting around them.

A rat darted past. Narseh almost shrieked as he saw it in the torchlight. Its ragged pelt was full of holes, exposing bones underneath. It was just as dead – and yet just as alive – as Wena's servants.

"What the fuck's going on down here?" he hissed.

"The necromantic energies," she said. "I told you they were building up. They can have some pretty weird side-effects."

"No kidding," said Narseh, trying to keep casual, even as chills ran down his spine. He caught himself squeezing her hand despite his best efforts and could only hope she didn't realise how anxious he was.

They hurried on as fast as the slow-moving treasure-laden zombies allowed, listening for sounds of pursuing mercenaries with axes. Finally, they emerged into a large, lightless sea-cave, which had been sealed off by those same long-ago pirates or smugglers to serve as a hideout. A wall of jagged rocks blocked the former cave entrance, with only a concealed door-way giving clandestine access to the jetty outside.

Where once the tide had come and gone, now a giant pool of stagnant water formed an underground lake, created by decades or centuries of accumulated sewer runoff. It reeked worse than anything Narseh had yet had the misfortune to smell, but he knew their boats, and their escape, waited just beyond it.

"Come on," he said, tugging at Wena's hand.

But she stood frozen to the spot, staring in horror at the stagnant pool.

Chapter 4: Anti-birth

"Don't. Move," whispered Wena.

Her senses warned her of some awful presence, something horrible and vast, lurking just under the surface. Some conglomeration of death, congealed perhaps from the corpses of rats or fish, insects, human hair, toenail clippings ... anything dead that had sluiced through the sewers to stew in this vile bath of necromantic miasma.

Whatever it was, it was no doubt inimical to life.

It was also, she knew for certain, impossible to control. Unlike zombies, created by formulaic spells passed down since the age before this one, the thing in the pool was a by-blow, a mutant.

She might've made it, albeit inadvertently, with the excessive energies that had spilled from her spells, but it sure wasn't hers to command.

"What's wrong?" asked Narseh.

"There's something in the water," she said, her voice low. "We have to be really, really quiet."

They crept around the edge of the pool, moving as silently as possible. The zombies moved quietly too, clasping the treasure chest between them. But the walkway was slick with putrescence, and wet from the lapping of the water, and Narseh's soft slippers were not made for such treacherous terrain. His feet slipped out from under him, and he fell arse-first toward the ground, upon which the coins stuffing his pockets seemed destined to make a great noisy CRASH.

Wena acted on instinct, calling on the power of her cloak. The strips of black shroud-cloth from which it was made came to writhing life and whipped around Narseh like the coils of an octopus, catching him mid-fall. The coins in his pockets clinked and jangled from the movement, and although the sounds were dim, they rang through the cavern regardless, like notes of distant music.

With her cloak, she set Narseh back on his feet. For once, he didn't seem to notice the putrid foulness of its fabric. Motionless, they stared at the water. Wena's heart raced as she saw a cluster of bubbles break the surface, heralding movement from below. She felt it, too, with her necromantic senses, the way a fisherman feels a quivering tension on his line when something has bitten below.

But was the thing in the water waking up, or merely rolling over in its sleep, stirred but not roused by the noise?

Tense, hideous moments passed as they watched the bubbles gradually cease. The thing remained dormant. Wena could sense its great quietude, pregnant with death.

She took a deep breath and released Narseh from the cloak. Holding hands again, they continued their silent course toward the exit. The slope leading up to it was crooked, rough, and coated in slime, looking even more treacherous than the walkway had been. Wena made for it regardless, but Narseh pulled her back, pointing to the zombies.

"They go first," he said. "I'm not letting that treasure chest out of my sight!"

Wena nodded to her butlers. They began climbing the slope with agonizing slowness, lugging the ungainly weight of the treasure chest between them. They were not elegant creatures at the best of times, and their burden, combined with the steepness of their ascent, and the slippery surface, was taxing their agility to the limit. Wena and Narseh watched and waited, glancing nervously between the zombies and the surface of the pool.

A bloodthirsty bellow echoed through the cavern as a na-ked corpse-painted axeman spattered with sawdust, rose petals, and blood came charging from the tunnel.

He'd reach them in no time! They had to escape – but the way was still blocked by the two shambling zombies!

"Do something!" urged Narseh.

"Like what?"

"I don't know, blast him with a lightning bolt!"

"I can't fucking do that!"

"You're a sorcerer!"

"That doesn't mean I have lightning powers!"

The axeman ran at them, skirting the edge of the pool. His bare feet had no problem at all negotiating the slippery slime; he was used to wading through entrails on the battlefield.

Wena looked again to the water, surprised to find herself actually hoping for bubbles. The creature within, whatever it was, was now their only hope of deliverance. Surely it would respond to the maniac's shouting!

But it didn't. Clearly, its slumber was deep. Below the wa-ters, the sounds of the mercenary's roars must have been muf-fled to a distant, humming vibration.

"Fuck!" whispered Wena.

The zombies were still only two-thirds of the way up, block-ing their escape. That giant axe came closer and closer, like a pendulum of death counting down. Desperately, Wena reached into her pocket and pulled out a diamond the size of a baby's clenched fist. She went to throw it into the water, thinking to stir up the beast, but Narseh held her back.

"Are you mad, woman? Use the lesser currencies!"

They both began tossing coins, sending ripples spreading across the surface in overlapping, colliding patterns, stirring currents that might disturb the monster beneath. Meanwhile, the axeman closed in, to fifty feet, then forty, then thirty –

Then stopped short as a monstrous mass reared up from the depths, streaming vile rivulets of stagnant water.

Dead things, she had thought, sluiced down into the sewers to fester and congeal in this awful cauldron, but what she saw now was not made up merely of rats, fish, and discarded toe-nail clippings. No, here were the unwanted bastards of the City of Whores, a host of half-formed embryos, myriad abortions brought together and melded into one by the necromantic energy tainting the cavern. Its overall appearance mirrored that of its integral parts, giving it the shape of a gigantic foetus with a translucent head and vestigial, rubbery features.

Still submerged to its navel, it loomed twenty feet above them. Only the zombies did not react with disgust; even Wena had to fight not to vomit at the sight or the stench of the abomination. She and Narseh huddled, clinging to each other, trembling and terrified.

The axeman froze for a moment, too, gaping with shock. Then he let out another war-cry, hefted his axe, and continued his charge toward Narseh, ignoring the beast.

It did not ignore him, but hurled itself onto the walkway with a great splash of rancid water, blocking his path and reaching for him with its flipper-like arms. Enraged, he swung at it, hacking so deep into its chest the full blade of his axe disappeared. Although he must have struck through to its hidden, awful heart, it only shuddered, then enfolded him in its grasp and embraced him to its bosom.

The gesture was essentially a hug, though not a very gentle one. The axeman shrieked, his bones pulverized as it squeezed. He went limp. His axe, dislodged, fell from his dead hands to vanish into the pool.

The creature shook him curiously, his body flopping like a broken doll. It then let out a thousand tiny anguished screams from the thousand tiny mouths that dotted its body.

Wena felt a tear dribbling from her eye. The monster may have been inimical to life – but perhaps all it wanted was love.

Mewling, it began to suck on Aktus' head as though it were a nipple.

"Looks like our friend's got a new job as a wet nurse," said Narseh, sounding as though he were trying to dampen down a tremor in his voice. "Let's get out of here, before it tries to suckle on us too!"

Wena's butlers were no longer blocking the ascent, so they ran for the exit and the jetty beyond, eager to hustle to their galleys and set off for brighter shores, leaving the plague-haunted city of Hedonia behind.

Chapter 10: Tales Within Tales

Some time later…

Narseh finished speaking and reclined on a pile of bright cushions, taking a draw from his hookah. Before him sat a very rich fool, his eyes wide with wonder.

"An amazing tale!" said the fool. "I almost can't believe it! First you arrive in Hedonia to help ferry desperate people away from the plague. Truly a noble endeavour! Then you uncover the existence of that nefarious brothel – what was it called – The Unwithering Flower? – which you discover is secretly being run by a necromancer, using magick to trick unsuspecting people into having sex with corpses! Who could conceive of such a repugnant, treacherous act? And on top of that, murdering beautiful young women to provide all the bodies? Ghastlier still! Yet you *still* took it upon yourself to infiltrate that whorehouse of horror and uncover those sickening shenanigans. You even managed to defeat the necromancer's axe-wielding henchmen, rescue the maiden they'd most recently kidnapped, and escape through that underground cove, bypassing the necromancer's pet monster by distracting it with coins. Truly a feat for the ages! But what, may I ask, happened next? What of all the gold and jewels you discovered in the necromancer's chamber? Were you able to keep any of it?"

Narseh sighed out smoke, and shook his head sadly.

"I'm afraid not," he said. "The maiden had swooned at the

sight of such horrors. I had to carry her delicate body to safety by myself, which meant I didn't have space in my arms for anything else. The rest was lost into that slime pit, to dwell with the monster forever. Thus, I returned to our glorious Alhazred poorer than ever, my coffers all but empty. The only treasure I managed to bring home from my journey was the maiden. Who, of course, became my seventh wife, so I still feel myself rich. For, surely, love is the greatest treasure of all. Wouldn't you agree?

"Indeed!" said the rich fool, looking enchanted. "Oh, Narseh, truly you're a man of courage and enlightenment! I'd like to offer you a gift in exchange for this incredible tale. Perhaps in such manner may the cruelties of fortune be somewhat reversed, and you'll receive the due thanks that your efforts deserve."

The fool gestured to his retinue of servants, who strode forth carrying armfuls of riches, including vessels of silver and gold, bolts of brocaded silk, and sacks of fine tobacco.

"Please allow this to replace a portion of the treasure you lost," said the fool.

"Ah, sir, You are too kind," said Narseh humbly inclining his head.

"Not at all! Though now I suppose I should leave you to your rest. You do have seven wives to satisfy, after all! But perhaps I could hear another of your amazing tales next week? If you've got time, that is…?"

"I think that could be arranged," said Narseh.

They rose, and bowed to each other, and the fool and his servants started filing from the chamber. As Narseh surveyed his new riches, a slave stepped forth from a discreet corner.

"Shall we put this with the rest of your treasure, master?" he asked.

Narseh slapped him over the head, hard. The sound of it echoed in the high-domed room.

"Idiot!" he hissed. "That gullible shithead might not yet be out of earshot!"

"Sorry, master," said the slave, who then waited for the sound of the villa's front door closing, and asked the same question again.

"Yes," said Narseh. "Now you may put this with the rest."

He unlocked his great vault and watched the slaves add the fresh pile of riches to the treasure horde inside.

His coffers were most definitely not empty, contrary to what he had told the rich fool. Nor was that the only lie or bent truth he'd told. Almost the whole story had been horribly distorted. For one thing, his seventh wife was no helpless young maiden from Hedonia, but an experienced woman from Khem.

And yet, there were a few grains of truth to the tale he'd just spun. He *had* rescued a woman from Hedonia, and she was surely virginal. For who could ever penetrate her body of glittering gold?

Narseh smiled at the golden statue of the courtesan crowning his treasure horde. Then, giving thanks to the Candle King, he dived into his coins like a pig into swill.

His seven wives would have to wait, as they so often did – the gold was calling his attentions tonight!

About the Author

B.J. Swann writes punk AF fiction with elements of fantasy, extreme horror, erotica, and anything else he wants to throw in there. The Aeon of Chaos is his fictional setting, a hyper-reality of fairytale madness where anything can happen.

Website: www.aeonofchaos.com

Contact: bjswann@aeonofchaos.com

By B.J. Swann and Elizabeth Bedlam

Holocaust Hearts

Two hearts bound across fathomless distance, haloed in fire that will murder the world.

A lot of devils are proud of Hell, but Silfer isn't one of them. He's bored with the torture and endless visceral depravity. He's bored with infernal politics. He's even bored with the charms of the lascivious succubus sisters – and that's really saying something. He's bored, he's bored, he's bored - and his secret, lonely heart is home to a fathomless longing.

Up on Earth, Mara is drowning in muted grey misery. She hates her job restoring antique books at the local museum. She hates the house-flipping yuppies who've infested her neighbourhood and made it so disgustingly trendy. She hates her busybody boss Kathy, who seems committed to making her life a misery with unwanted friendship. With a longing both nameless and consuming she dreams of something far beyond her daily banality.

One day she recieves a box of mouldering books from the bowels of a faraway church. Nestled like refuse amongst the tomes are a series of loose pages made from calfskin – or something very like it. They speak to her in whispers and hell-fire dreams. Unbenowkst to Mara, she's stumbled on the lost pages of the *Codex Infernalis Futuatis*, the most terrible book ever to be released from the gates of Hell. As Silfer seeks the book, his world collides with Mara's, and their hearts become bound in a love that will forever devour them both – and have terrible consequences of the rest of the universe.

From the combined pens of Elizabeth Bedlam, queen of offbeat erotic horror, and B.J. Swann, creator of the Aeon of Chaos, Holocaust Hearts is a black romantic comedy steeped in carnage, depravity, and total hilarity. You've never read anything like it.

Also by B.J. Swann

Our Lady of the Scythe

"Hogwarts and Camp Halfblood, move the HELL over; there's a new boarding school in town and it is **not** for the kiddies!" - Christine Morgan, Splatterpunk Award-winning author of Lakehouse Infernal

Eighteen-year-old Raza has a problem. Every time she tries to get busy with a boy, she turns into a monster and tears him apart. Why? Because her father is the Big Horned Bastard, demon supreme. To unlock the mysteries of her birthright - and hopefully get some sex education - she's sent to Our Lady of the Scythe, a boarding school for demon-spawn where detention is a realm of flesh-eating monsters and the delinquents get their kicks out of mass murder. Will she even survive the first semester? And what happens when she and her new friends stumble on a vile angelic plot that threatens the survival of all demonkind? Raza will have to embrace her inner demon fast, or kiss her butt goodbye.

Our Lady of the Scythe: Demon Academy is a Punk As Fuck riff on the supernatural boarding school genre. It contains graphic sex, violence, and potentially disturbing material. It is not intended for children or the easily offended.

Also by B.J. Swann

The Crimson Crown

Inverted Dreams. Excoriated Hearts. Terror and Horror Sublime.

The twin princesses Oda and Honey are as different as night and day. Oda is a child of the dark, obsessed with cruelty and death. Honey is as sweet as her name, filled with goodwill and compassion. It is therefore a remarkably revolting twist of fate when the royal astrologer orders Oda to be married to the mild-mannered King Armand, while Honey is betrothed to King Barbus of Gutgirt, the most brutal man in the world, who tears peasants apart with his bare hands and keeps his murdered brides' bodies on display in his own bloody chamber.

As the twins strive to wrest back their lives from the cruel hand of fate, they embark on a journey of self discovery that will twist them in unimaginable ways – and perhaps bare the secrets of their innermost selves. At the centre of their struggles, shining balefully over all, is the Crimson Crown of Gutgirt, a relic of terrible mystery and demonic power, whose secrets hold the key to salvation – and everlasting doom.

The Crimson Crown is a Punk as Fuck fantasy story set in the Aeon of Chaos. It contains graphic sex, violence, and potentially disturbing material. It is not intended for children or the easily offended.

Also by B.J. Swann

The Court of the Mushroom King

Psychedelic strangeness. Demonic romance. Total mayhem.

In the kingdom of Myconia lies a forbidden garden filled with mushrooms whose flesh is said to bring ecstatic visions to some, to others a fate worse than death. Princess Ziqqora, whose only passion is dreaming, resolves to taste the illicit fungus and discover the truth. She finds herself in a realm of terror and wonder beyond even her wildest imaginings, a place filled with inhuman enemies and marvelous allies – allies who might just be able to save her from her doomed fate as the intended bride of the murderous Heinrich van Gruel and the monster he keeps in his codpiece.

The Court of the Mushroom King is a Punk as Fuck fantasy story set in the Aeon of Chaos. It contains graphic sex, violence, and potentially disturbing material. It is not intended for children or the easily offended.

Also by B.J. Swann

The Second Wolf

Bestial Violence. Monstrous Lust. Total Mayhem.

A Beast stalks the forests and moors around the city of Stubbe, raping and killing by night, vanishing by day. As the bodies of mangled victims pile up, the citizens grow increasingly terrified – and violent. Unable to stop or trap the elusive Beast, or fathom the cause of its inhuman lusts, the local constabulary is forced to seek help from an outsider in the form of Rubria Caracalla, a beautiful monster hunter of vague but lethal reputation. But Rubria is no ordinary monster hunter, and her perverted plans for the Beast are not the same as those of her patrons.

"The Second Wolf" is a Punk as Fuck fantasy story set in the Aeon of Chaos. It contains graphic sex, violence, and potentially disturbing material. It is not intended for children or the easily offended.

Available exclusively from www.godless.com